Trademark of Random House, Inc., William Collins Sons & Co. Ltd., Authorised User

THE BEAR FAIR

by Stan and

9 10

ISBN 0 00 171315 9 (paperback)
ISBN 0 00 171162 8 (hardback)

Copyright © 1975 by Stanley and Janice Berenstain
A Beginner Book published by arrangement with
Random House Inc., New York, New York
First published in Great Britain 1976

Printed in Great Britain by
William Collins Sons & Co Ltd, Glasgow

DETECTIVES

THE CASE OF THE MISSING PUMPKIN.

Jan Berenstain

COLLINS

THE BEAR DETECTIVES

Will they solve the case?

Farmer Ben

Will he get his pumpkin back?

The Missing Pumpkin

Where can it be?

The Spooky Stranger

Who can it be?

Papa Bear
and Snuff

Will they
be much help?

Will the Bear Detectives get their bear?

Help!
My pumpkin won
first prize at the fair.
Now I can't find it
anywhere!

Do not worry,
Farmer Ben.
The BEAR DETECTIVES
will find it again!

Your prize pumpkin stolen?
Never fear.
Great Bear Detective Pop is here!
I will find it.
You will see.

Just watch
my old dog Snuff and me.

But, Papa,
our Bear Detective Book
will tell us how
to catch the crook.

"Lesson One.
First look around
for any TRACKS
that are on the ground."

Don't waste your time
with books and stuff!
We're on the trail!
Just follow Snuff!

We'll catch that crook.
We'll show you how.
Snuff and I
will catch the . . .

. . . cow?

Say! Look down there!
Do you see what I see?

There's a
WHEELBARROW TRACK
going by this tree!

A good detective
writes things down:

"Checked out a cow,
white and brown."

The track ends here.
What shall we do?

We'll look in the book.

It says,
"Lesson Two.
Look all around
for another clue."

Humf! You can look around
as much as you please.
I'm going to follow
these carrots and peas . . .

. . . and eggshells
and corncobs
and other stuff.

This must be the way!
Let's go, Snuff!

MUNCH MUNCH CRUNCH GOBBLE

Listen, Snuff!
Hear that munching?
That pumpkin thief is
pumpkin lunching!

O.K., thief!
You've munched your last.
Your pumpkin-stealing
days are past.

Look here! Look here,
Papa Bear.
We found a new clue
over there.

You see
we found
a PUMPKIN LEAF . . .

Aha!
You've found a pumpkin leaf.
Just show me where
you found this leaf.
Then I will find that
pumpkin thief.

The pumpkin thief!
I've found him, Snuff!
Let's grab him quick.
He sure looks tough.

Be careful, Pop.
Lesson Three in the book
says, "Before you leap,
be sure to look."

Hang on, Snuff!
Hold him tight!
This pumpkin thief
can really fight.

Did you find any clues
in that scarecrow, Pop?
Shall we keep on looking,
or shall we stop?

Hmmmmmmmmm . . .
Checked out a cow,
three pigs in a pen,
and a scarecrow owned
by Farmer Ben.

Found some tracks
and a pumpkin leaf.
Still haven't found
that pumpkin thief.

Look! By that haystack!
I see something blue!
It's the first-prize ribbon.
That's a very good clue!

A haystack!
The perfect place
to hide.

I'll bet the thief
is right inside.

Pumpkin thief,
don't try to run.
Your pumpkin-stealing
days are done!

But, Papa . . .

I was trying to say,
I don't think the thief
is in THAT hay.

Hmmmmmm . . .
Ben's haystack
is another spot
where the pumpkin thief
is not.

Say! Look over there!
Look in that door!
PUMPKIN SEEDS
all over the floor!

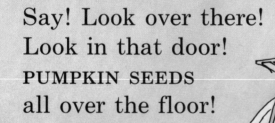

He's in the barn! This is it!
Hand me that detective kit.

I'll snap on these handcuffs.
I'll take him to jail.
Pumpkin thief,
it's the end of the trail.

Old Snuff,
this may be tough.

It looks
like we've caught
a whole GANG
of crooks.

Hmmmmm . . .
Checked out a cow,
brown and white.
Checked out a scarecrow
after a fight.

Checked out a haystack.
Three pigs in a pen . . .
Put the cuffs on
Farmer Ben's hen.

Found some tracks,
a ribbon, a leaf . . .
some pumpkin seeds,

BUT STILL
NO THIEF!

Small Bear, I guess you better look
at what it says there in your book.

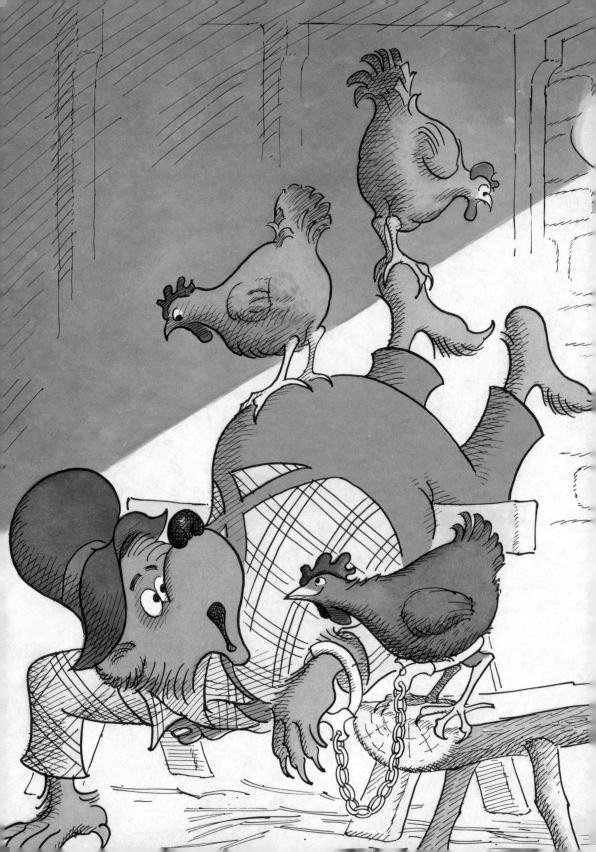

Lesson Four—
here's how it goes—
"A good detective
will USE HIS NOSE!"

Hmmmmmmm . . .
Pumpkin seeds,
pumpkin shell—
and . . .
aha!
I smell a
PUMPKIN SMELL!

The pumpkin was pied
by Mrs. Ben.

The case is solved.
Good work, men!
The BEAR DETECTIVES
have done it again!

MMMMMMM!
My dear, you and I
will SHARE first prize.
ME for the pumpkin,
YOU for the pies!